unapologetically

SYDNEY WELLS

Book Vine Press
2516 Highland Dr.
Palatine, IL 60067

Acknowledgments
Beautifully Broken

Prologue

I have endured by the grace of God and not by any intelligence on my part. I lost my mother at the age of nine to a drug overdose and was sent to live with my paternal grandfather and his wife. I had a hard time learning what love looked like. My mother was always busy with the nature of her boyfriend turned husband's odds and ends in the world of drugs. That resulted in me visiting my grandfather or aunt on weekends. There was never any time for mother, daughter. Frankly, I was in the way of my mother of enjoying her anticyclones.

My mother gave birth to me at the age of fifteen, she and I were branded in the eyes of the community and stiff neck Christians.

The only sign of love I saw was when my grandfather talked to his wife and the way, he would touch her the tenderness and the way he would hold her while he kissed her hello or goodbye.

My aunt was self-spoiled and wanted everything for herself and it had to be her way at whatever cost. After I was born, my mother's sister would needle her for not continuing her high school education or going to their prom. They were twins and my mother's sister had continuously made everything between them a competition.

My mother was defensive about everything, and that became increased anger about anything. My mother eventually married her worthless drug runner, who spent more time in jail than at home. My mother would go with him sometimes leaving me with my grandfather to worry if she would come back.

The journey that took them from Illinois to Missouri was a dangerous one. Mother was miserable and unhappy, yet she insisted on living her life full of highs and lows.

I entered a private Christian school and was taught about a man named Jesus. This man was sent to save the people of God! So, I thought what is wrong with my mother, aunts, grandmother, and nosy neighbors? In my view, they missed that big time!

I had a habit of asking a lot of questions and the teacher would be intolerant of me and my insistence of knowing this truth being sold to us kids!

There were angels guiding people, opening gates, dropping chains off arms and legs just because they were singing and praising God? Three men go into a fire and do not get burned!!? This is some strange stuff! I have questions on how can this be??

I am now sixteen years old and have had no love, phenomenal happenings, where is this God/Jesus? No one asked me to the junior or senior prom how sad is that? There is this new boy in school, and I like him much.

He has a car he is a senior and handsome. Will he ever notice me?

At lunch one of my friends told him and he started looking at me every day at school but says nothing. How long does it take to find and understand real love?

Now, I am seventeen graduating high school and I have my first boyfriend he is handsome, thoughtful, he stole my heart, or did I just fall for the first? We married.

Chapter I

Jessie and I are complicated we understand each other but we are not on the same page. Jessie is an insurance salesman with The Guidance Life Company. Jessie is a man of the need it now cannot wait for its group. Whereas I am the let us save and afford it a practical group. Looking at Jessie sometimes I would wonder what if I had waited for this love.

Could there have been another more suitable and tolerable? Jessie is six feet tall, almond skin, curly dusty brown hair, big brown eyes, big lips, and a charming personality all in one package. However, this man will not pick up after himself, move a plate to the sink, take the trash out, put his underwear into the dirty clothes bin, his clothes usually end up at the foot of the bin. He has never been available to help me with anything.

After we married, we moved into an awesome cottage in Madison, Wisconsin. The days were long and happy. Seems like yesterday.

Jessie had an eye for nice things. I did too but I wanted to purchase a dream home in a few years. He would buy new suits for work two-three times a month. Expensive tailor-made suits. I like Michael Kors but would rather save until we secure a home and start a family. Jessie came home with a new car after he earned a big bonus from Guidance Life.

We argued all evening. I yelled how could you without discussing it with me first or allowing me to be a part of the purchase. Jessie gave a typical answer. This is my bonus and I will spend it any way I want; you are not my boss! Of course, I cried and tried to explain to him that we had made plans together we wanted a great future, family, and retirement. After I looked at the car papers. "Jessie", I yelled you brought a sixty-thousand-dollar car!! How are we going to pay for this? He looked at me as if to say "I didn't think about that?!

I work at Fisher Investments; I am an accountant of all careers to have with this man. We both make decent salaries and can move forward quickly. Jessie likes the fast life and all it has to offer. Jessie feels like we should live off my salary and he should do whatever he wants with his salary. Jessie worked with a well-dressed man Arthur J. Cason "Art", as we called him. Art was the know it all man. He went on expensive trips around the globe and drove luxurious cars. Art's home was beyond stunning with marble floors, state of the art kitchen, servants, a swimming pool, and a gated driveway.

Jessie and I were guests at Art's home several times. His third wife seemed a little out of weird for Art. Art is about five feet three, black and grey hair, with matching beard, receding hairline, skin like an orange, and a smooth talker. Art can be annoying with his know-it-all about everything. His wife Kaylee was at least fifteen years younger, quiet, obedient, and pretty. Kaylee is about five feet tall, in great shape, hazel eyes, short black hair, and she dresses only in Prada and has no talent for holding a conversation.

Jessie loves this man and wants the same things as Art. This makes no sense at all. Material things are alright, but you plan for them not to spend and generate debt to make an impression on someone. How is Art doing this anyway?

Jessie comes home telling me we are going to Las Vegas for the weekend. Las Vegas, I asked? Yes, Jessie says Art is taking us on his uncle's private plane. Okay, now I can understand somethings about Art. However, I do not like Art or his wife. Flying over Las Vegas was beautiful the lights and landscape were a work of art. After we landed, a limousine took us to the Waldorf Astoria. The ride was beautiful on way to the hotel this was an unexpected seat in luxury and the gratification I had never experienced. This entire trip was sponsored by Art and Kaylee. I hope I enjoy the trip because I do not like these sponsors.

This is some serious VIP stuff; we did not have to check into the hotel the staff was waiting for us. They were grouped outside the hotel curbside, and at the lobby entrance. Once inside our room for a minute, I lost my breath. The view was awesome overlooking the Monte

Carlo Hotel and swimming pool. The bathroom was fit for royalty Granite floors and counters. The bathtub was deep and shaped to fit on a saucer. The room was gold, white, and black. I could stay in this room the whole trip and be extremely happy with room service of course. Jessie did not even give me time to unpack or freshen up before he is out the door calling for me to hurry up. Art's waiting downstairs. I dropped everything and went reluctantly. As soon as we exited the elevator there was Art and Kaylee! Let us go says Art with the grin of a devil.

We were driven in a limousine to the Colosseum at Caesars Palace for a Mariah Carey concert. We just walked into section one-zero-four in the front and had one of the best seats in the place. We continuously passed any obstacles and sauntered right into our places! No tickets, no IDs, no credit cards just straight to the appointed time, and place.

After the concert, we dined at Twist by Pierre Gagnaire in our hotel. Art says it will be close to his room and bed after drinking.

I watched Jessie all night and saw him taking mental notes of Art, his demeanor, and stature. I took mental notes of my own, about Art, I was looking at a man with no class, show-off, phony, fake wants us too to believe he is all that. There is a little man behind the curtain! He just has a big voice to deceive who he is.

Breakfast was at the Palace Station Hotel & Casino. This lifestyle is boring.

There is no laughter, fun, or mingling with others. Art and Kaylee seem to stay to themselves and have shut out others from their lives completely. Kaylee and I have only said three words between us. The conversations were between Jessie and Art and always Art's knowledge of business and the ways to get rich.

That evening I asked Jessie the reason for this trip, he looked at me as if I am unappreciative of even being invited. Jessie walked out of the room and went to shower.

I began to search my theories on Art, and what was going on. Here in this beautiful room and the lighted city no romance, no holding hands no candlelight dinners, no night strolls, no exploring the events, and even a little drinking. What is the point!

On the way home Art was watching me. Every time I would look in his direction, he was looking at me. I could see him in my peripheral vision gawking like an eagle ready to strike. Art knows I did not like him, and I know his speeches are full of holes. A nobody trying hard to be somebody.

One thing I know is rich people who worked hard or inherited what they have do not show off. The ones who like the press and social media do not stay to themselves.

Arriving home, I was exhausted the fun trip was just a trip. Because I was tripping the whole time. Jessie was quiet and I could tell his wheels was rolling. What now and how is this going to help, hurt, or destroy our home.

I noticed a change in Jessie. He was moody and short-tempered. Our budget was out the door and no need for me to say anything no need for an argument that I would lose anyway.

These past few weeks Jessie has not come straight home from work. My cooking is in vain. So, I would stop by Chick-fil-A and get myself dinner. Eating alone had become an expected norm.

I decided to do a little investigation on Jessie. I went up to the Global Life Building to see for myself what he was doing. I purposely made it at the lunch hours so I can explain I wanted to take him to lunch.

Chapter 2

I entered the building, and this was my first time coming here in a year. The guard did not recognize me I showed him my ID and he apologized and said go on up no need for me to call and announce you.

I took the elevator to the thirty-fifth floor and stepped off into a sea of insurance investigators, regulators claim adjustors and policy writers. I scanned the floor for a familiar face or two. None I could see from the past. So, I walked toward Jessie's office and just as I turned the corner there was Eleanor a beautiful sight to see. She was surprised and extremely glad to see me. Eleanor was Jessie's executive assistant. She was always trying to get me to come to her church and I always had an excuse why I could not make it. Yet she constantly showed love and concern for Jessie and

I. Eleanor had me sit down and tell her how I have been. I summed it up as I am losing Jessie and do not know what to do. Eleanor said take it to Jesus and He will tell you what to do. I told her I have a hard time with this Jesus can fix anything. I said the miracles, the marvels, the saving grace, come on. Tell me the miracles you have had! Know any blind men who can see now? Any lame who can walk now? Eleanor looked with sadness and said I am praying for you to know the Lion of Juda and see him face to face. Now Eleanor says how can I help you. Jessie, I said where is Jessie? He went to lunch with Mr. Arthur Cason, Eleanor said.

May I confide in you Eleanor I asked. Sure, Eleanor said what is it? I do not like Art at all he is a menace and a danger to me and my husband. Art takes all of Jessie's time and I am alone. I came here today to find out what is going on.

Eleanor dropped her head and started praying. I was turned off until she said to bless the marriage and if it is not of your will reveal it and leave no doubt.

Any interference in this marriage break off the hand. Eleanor had tears in her eyes!

She looked at me and said child get to the Word of God, and life of Jesus, and you will understand what is in front of you and what is about to be before you. You need a shield and the only shield that will protect you is the shield of Faith covered by the blood of Jesus. Then and only then can you suit up with the armor of God. I was puzzled at the emotional evidence of tears from Eleanor. I hugged her and thanked her for her support mentally and spiritually.

Little did I know Eleanor saw in the spirit what was going to happen to me. She had already pleaded my case to her Lord!

Arriving home, I felt funny and alone the kind of alone that is empty, void of being. I showered changed clothes and sat down with a cup of tea. Reminiscing today's events.

I am missing something that is right in front of my face. Eleanor was steadfast in her prayer and gave me a warning of sorts. I just cannot put my finger on it.

Jessie came home at eleven-thirty. What the hell Jessie I said? He looked at me and said I had things to do. Like what I asked? It does not concern you ok, it does not concern you. That was the longest night ever.

Jessie started staying out after work later and later. I do not know how to handle this situation! Who can I talk to? I need some advice, counsel. I do not want to lose my mind.

After crying for a little over a month I decided to call Eleanor and set up a meeting. Eleanor said it is Wednesday night prayer and I should come, and we can talk afterward.

I was reluctant but went anyway. There I was at the Christian Community Church. To my surprise, there were about seventy-five people here on a Wednesday night! I sat in the back in case I need to make a quick exit.

The Pastor was a woman I was shocked and amazed. She taught from the book of Romans Chapter twelve A Living Sacrifice. I listened with intent and she explained it perfectly. I understood what she was teaching. I had no questions!

Wow was all I could think, and I enjoyed the way she handled the scriptures and her examples were on point.

Eleanor and I walked around the block to a little café and had coffee. I told her Jessie was not coming home at night. Eleanor asked me what his demeanor was like. I could only say mean, non-talkative, and distant. Eleanor prayed for me and advised I get into the church to grow strong in the Word with the protection of the Lord. Eleanor saw something I can tell however she said nothing.

I started going to church on Sundays and met nice, kind people. The pastor showed me love and made me feel a part of the family there.

One evening while doing laundry I found a needle in Jessie's pocket. What in the world was this doing in his pocket? Everything started to click, missing spoons Jessie's mood swings, late nights, and broke all the time. I confronted Jessie, and as expected denial and lies. Finally, I pulled out the needle. Jessie broke and admitted he has developed a problem. How? I asked him how did this happen? Art had a party and they were doing a variety of feel-good drugs. Feel good I yelled what do you mean to feel good?

Jessie became belligerent and left the house he was gone three days. I would not have been able to get through this without my newfound church family. I am growing stronger than ever.

The bank account is dwindling hundreds gone. So, I closed it and opened one in my name only. Jessie was so mad now what am I supposed to do? Open an account for yourself and do what you do I said. Just when I thought I had a handle on things, household items started missing. To make matters worse Jessie got fired.

The house and car notes, insurance, and utilities that were formed for two incomes have now become the burden on one income, mine! I now hide my purse and anything of value. Last night I put my purse on the at the head of the bed on the floor. About midnight I heard a constant tapping. I opened my eyes not moving to hear what was making that sound. I rose up and to my surprise, there was Jessie with a broom lying on his stomach trying to reach my purse on my side of the bed! I screamed for him to get out and grabbed my purse. Jessie was sleeping on the couch because he had a hard time bathing.

Arriving home after stopping at the grocery store. I parked in the garage walked to the kitchen put down my bags, showered, and put on comfy clothes. I started dinner for myself but felt funny, a little strange something was out of sorts. I proceeded to put a chicken in the top oven and cornbread in the bottom oven. Corn and green beans on the stove. Then a light went on! I turned around and the ceiling fan with lights was gone. This was the moment I was deciding where am I at in this unfolding drama.

It has been a year and Jessie has been on again off again. We have not been as a married couple in months. He said he would go to the doctor for help. Jessie was told he had a prostate issue and it could be fixed. Three months later Jessie was given Viagra. I would ask did it work Jessie would say no. After two months we went back to the doctor and he was given Cialis again I would ask is it working? No, he would answer. So now I am suspicious about the whole thing. I ran into Kaylee at Nordstrom's I was returning a dress a brought six months ago, to get money back. Kaylee was Prada shopping with her unlimited charge card. I asked her if she knew anything about Jessie and his habit. To my surprise, she told me Art had drug parties every week. Jessie would trade some pills he had for Heroin. She did not know what kind of pills they were, but I did.

Hurt and realizing this marriage is not working. I have gone to drug meetings alone and with Jessie. I have stood and said I am an enabler in front of people with the same issues. Yet I am getting hurt and there is a dark cloud over me.

That following Wednesday night at church a woman came up to me and said I was Victorious, and I would defeat the enemy with great victory as it was with Daniel. Then she said I declare and decree it to be so!

I was taken back and puzzled, however, I except those words concerning me. I was feeling something in the pit of my being.

I want to know more about this prophetic message. I needed that to encourage me, due to my situation, I need triumphs in my life.

Jessie is gone days at a time, I wonder if he is alive. With overdoses, and the game of getting money to purchase drugs at any cost was a bit unnerving. I am learning to trust the one that is greater in me.

While cleaning the bedroom I found a plastic bag from the cleaners on the floor under Jessie's suits. Wondering

what this was from and why was it on the floor.
take long for me to figure out it was from my
He took it! I steamed for three days before I was able
talk, yell, and let my frustration out! Jessie was home when
I returned from work. I lit into him as soon as I saw him.
"WHERE IS MY FUR"!!! Jessie tried to explain with the
look bae I before he could finish, I shut him down. Jessie,
I said while clenching my teeth I better have my fur in the
closet tomorrow, or you better go into protective custody!
I stormed into the bedroom and ran bathwater with extra
bubbles. That way I can soak and cry.

Never did I ever dream this would happen to me this
way with the man I trusted. Now I hide everything and
anything of value. Yet somehow, he seems to find it. Jessie
spent hours in the bathroom and when he would exit the
smell was something I never experienced. Later to find out
it was the burning tar on small spoons I was missing from
my flatware. The closer I get to Jesus His Word and promises
the worse my home life seems to become. What am I doing
wrong? I believed I had the best husband, with the biggest
heart, all I have is the biggest horror!

I called Eleanor and asked if she can help me understand
these scriptures and know why they do not apply to me and
my situation? Eleanor was excited to meet with me. She had
been trying for several years to get me to celebrate her church
and learn of Christ. I was mean and would smile with the
thought of no intent to do any such thing. Now, look at
me about to go through the same things from elementary

school asking the questions I had then and never found or was told the answers to my questions. I had a hard heart against the Christian movement period!

Eleanor met me at the Sims Café she had a beautiful glow about her with salt & pepper hair she was stunning. Eleanor must be in her late sixties she has grandchildren with children. She is petite, eloquent, kind, and genteelly persistent all the while smiling with a true sense of love and wanting to connect.

I thanked Eleanor for meeting with me on such an early Saturday morning. After going over all the details with Eleanor I was exhausted. Yet she listened to my every word and showed concern for me. Was I beginning to understand what a true Christian looks like?

Each day seems like a long year, long dark and isolated. I have made myself inaccessible to co-workers and neighbors. embarrassed about my marriage and what I am not doing about it.

Sleep is not obtainable, my heart cries out for a solution and end to this madness.

Sunday morning seemed different to me there was a newness to the sun on my face as I backed out of the garage. The ride to church was pleasant I forgot about my problems and focused on the praise and worship praying for an answer to everything through the sermon a Word for me Lord please a Word for me.

I pulled into the parking lot some beautiful sisters and brothers were coming to worship this morning and get a Word for the Lord like me. I parked and made my way into the sanctuary. After sitting down the choir came in and the praise and worship began. My heart was so full and wanted desperately to hear from the God, Lord, and Holy Spirit I have heard so much about. Although I could not wrap my head around all the Bible lessons of God and His Son. However, I am more than willing to lay down my doubts and move on to this unknown adventure with all the discoveries. Making known the unknown to me I WANT TO BELIEVE I need a God in my life to show me the way! I want all the glorious miracles, life-changing events, and the walk on water faith. The pastor came from the book of Genesis, Romans, and Mark. I listened with all my heart. The message was God formed us.... Sin deformed us.... Christ Transformed us.... and the master transformer. Sin? I understand sin! Simple right from wrong, sin the opposite of God's Will and commandments the New Testament rules to follow. Love your enemies.

I asked Eleanor after service what do I do now? I believe God is my creator His Son as my Redeemer and the Holy Spirit Christ left here for us to rely on. Eleanor smiled and said "baby" you need to be baptized. I was baptized on the first Sunday and my life changed. I was learning with the help of Bible study to pray and have faith that my prayers would be answered according to the will of the Father God.

I started praying at midnight because of the glory and righteousness of God. Like the song says, "in the midnight hour Gods going to turn it around". A few weeks later I started praying and ordering my day before the sun rose. Six months later Jessie came to me and asked to go to a rehab center to get clean. Wow was I amazed and happier than I have ever been in my marriage.

Jessie went into the New Hope Opioid Addiction Center. There Jessie spent twenty-four weeks. I was not allowed to talk or see him for the first six weeks. I prayed for Jessie.

Time sped by and I was on my way to pick-up Jessie. He looked so good and fresh. On the way home, we had a decent conversation. I was excited to tell him about the Lord and how He changed my life. Jessie listened but there was no reaction on anything I had said.

That night as I rose to pray at midnight, I had a vision thick white clouds were surrounding me. They were thick and still, suddenly a violent wind came but the clouds kept me safe. I was amazed and I did not know the meaning of my open vision.

Jessie wanted to see Art and insisted on visiting Art. Art! I said why would you even want to be in the same room with that guy. Jessie said I need to tell him how I feel. Jessie went to see Art and was gone the entire evening. When Jessie returned home, he was distant and seemed occupied mentally. I went to bed and Jessie fell asleep on the couch.

What is going on? I am pressing into my Father for answers. The spirit within tells me darkness has returned and beware conditions are not right in here.

Jessie's been home for two weeks. He had not inquired about a job, or even looked for one. Sleeping late and up-all-night making trips to Art's three and four times a week. I am trusting God in every way I know-how. I have prayed for my husband, and myself. I asked for a Holy Spirit Home and children. Faith, Faith is what I am holding on to!

Saturday morning Jessie comes to the kitchen with this big grin and hugs me tightly. Wow, I thought what brought this on out of nowhere. Babe, Jessie says

I want to take you on a "New Beginning" awesome vacation! Vacation? Jessie, we cannot afford a vacation. Jessie looked so hurt and held me tighter. "Please," he said to me please let me do this for us, you and me!

I was baffled about this how, where, when, and how much the cost will be? I sat down at the kitchen table and asked Jessie how are you going to do this?

Jessie kneeled in front of me and said…just then I heard a cry small faint cry gentle as if a newborn was awakened from his sleep hungry. Art's is paying for the whole trip: we will not need to pay for anything. "What"! Jessie, have you forgotten what this man has done to you? Please Jessie kept saying over and over. Tell me why Jessie Why I asked. He is sorry and wants to make it to you and me. So, Art is paying for a get-a-way for us I asked? Well, not exactly for us but includes us. Oh, no not so fast Jessie I said as I raised my voice an octave. You need to start explaining what is going on and do not leave out any details!

Art wants to show you and me a wonderful time and have an awesome experience. Art wants to take us on a safari.

When I hear Jessie say safari, I choked a little and gasp for air. I could not even answer for a minute or so. Are you kidding me Jessie for real? You would go on a safari and with Art? Yes! Yes, I would Jessie said this is a lifetime experience! I told Jessie I had to think about it.

That night as I had laid in bed my ceiling opened. I saw white clouds in a circle and black windy clouds were trying to penetrate the circle of white clouds. Soon the black windy clouds disintegrated in failure to infiltrate the white circle. I was in awe of the vision and look for the meaning. That morning was beautiful and the sun rays on my face were inviting and smiling. I feel good and decided to give Jessie support and allow Art to give us a vacation.

Jessie was like a little kid waiting for Christmas it was all he talked about. Art let us know we were going to Zimbabwe and will stay at a campsite. I am just not excited about this African trip at all. Looking back at all that had transpired I was grateful to the Father for the strength and ability to move forward and most of all showing me the way to His heart with a greater understanding of what TRUTH is. From darkness to light, blindness to sight, I am climbing and standing on a solid rock of faith. Zimbabwe you are part of God's creation. Jessie says out trip is in three weeks and we need some light clothes and hats for the weather there with the average temperature of eighty-three degrees. Hot, dry, sunny, and sweaty.

Jessie brought our flight tickets and itinerary I was hesitant to even look at it however, I did with a frowned face.

I was saddened to see a twenty-two hour, thirty-five-minute flight going with Ethiopian Airlines making two stops. Then going on too Harare, Zimbabwe, where we will spend one night at the Harare Safari Lodge. Then travel to the Kanga camp Zimbabwe

What in the world am I going to do in the air for twenty-two hours and thirty-five minutes I thought to myself, then I had to chuckle. Read the Word, listen to the Word, place myself into the Word, and sleep on the Word. I have so many questions of the Lord what a great time to investigate and inquire of my Father! After, all I will be thirty-five thousand feet in the air that is close to heaven I thought while laughing. I can touch the hand of God. So now I am excited about this adventure.

Chapter 3

The plane was quiet, and Jessie traded seats with Kaylee sitting with Art they babbled on for hours. Kaylee sat in a vacant seat keeping to herself.

I was amazed that I was able to give myself to prayer, reading, and meditation without interruptions.

Looking out at the huge white clouds they seem to dance and praise, what is this with clouds? What was the meaning and why? I began reading in the Book of Daniel what an awesome soul he was. Deciding to worship God only at all costs. I felt so encouraged by his story. While reading the Book Daniel I felt a real connection to the story and all the characters. Especially Daniel being good looking, with wisdom and intelligence, gifted with dream interpretations, something I would like to have.

My eyes had become heavy and after we were served dinner, I fell asleep. I fell into a deep sleep. Suddenly the airplane shook with great violence. I opened my eyes not knowing what to expect! There in front of me was a sunlight bright cloud I could not look at it, it blinded me. The warmth was felt to my soul. There came a voice from the cloud with the intensity of thunder saying, "I am with you always"!

I woke up and felt refreshed, yet I am puzzled for the meanings, however overjoyed that the Father knows me and was with me on this journey.

I could not help but wonder if I would witness to the natives and bring them to God through Jesus. What is the path set before me?

We arrived at Harare International Airport and had a limousine take us to the Harare Safari Lodge. There we stayed one night to rejuvenate from the long flight. Jessie and I were in a room that stood alone somewhat like a hut on the dirt ground and net all around the room. We were able to enjoy air conditioning, indoor bathroom, and a shower, before going to the safari camp.

That night I felt in my spirit that Jessie was distant and did not engage in conversation no matter how hard I tried to talk with him.

The tour ranger came for us at six p.m. wow, I thought it is a seven-hour difference here. We gathered our things and headed out to the Land Rover.

That took us to the Kanga Camp Zimbabwe called by some "the armchair safari". It was incredible an oasis in the middle of a jungle.

There was a beautiful wooden carved table draped with a white tablecloth along with matching chairs, the dining was set for four. Wine glasses, red wine, elegant dishes with napkins on the plates, and a beautiful candle encased in a tall wooden holder. We dined on a riverbank the camp is set on the riverbank!

To my surprise twenty feet away there were elephants! Black, Brown from the mud and red elephants! I counted eight large and five small babies. They were drinking and standing in the water. They remained calm and peaceful the entire time, before moving on. I could not eat properly for gazing at these magnificent animals. I was speechless. Retiring to our lodging I was so full of what I saw and admired I tried to get some conversation out of Jessie but all I got was umm, yea and I know. Then I remembered at dinner Jessie and Art were locked into a conversation. Kaylee was not impressed she ate and retired never saying a word.

The next morning our two African Bush Camp Guides took us on a wildlife drive. Kaylee did not come out. We left without her. I must have taken one-hundred pictures. There before me were giraffes, zebras, monkeys of several varieties, and some leopards.

Just then I felt the Spirit come over me most amazingly. Holding my breath and using my strength I asked what is it, Lord?

I looked back and saw the gravel from the jeep raise higher and higher from the dirt road. We were going faster and faster. Just then I noticed Art and the two guides were friendly like they knew each other. It was just about dusk dark and suddenly we stopped. Art said to me you been taken a lot of pictures. The guide says there are baby elephants just beyond the bushes. Get some good shots and you will be able to get them on National Geographic's. Everyone laughed. No, I am good I said, then Jessie said come on I will go with you.

Are you serious Jessie? Jessie looked at me and said yes this will be a lifetime shoot. Baby elephants with their mothers. Jessie jumped out of the jeep and extended his hand to me and helped me down.

We walked down the small slope toward the bushes and rapidly Jessie let go of me and jumped back into the jeep!

I stood there watching the jeep go down the road until it was out of sight. It was dusk dark, and I was nervous and alone in the wildlife preserve. I walked to the bushes as most elephants are not dangerous.

To my, surprise a lion came out he roared and slowly walked toward me. I saw his enormous paws with claws his eyes had anger in them and a meal on his mind, as three other lions all-male from the mane on their heads walked behind the first lion. I said if I am to die so be it. The lion jumped me knocking me down his weight was crushing he clawed my neck and opened his mouth to devour me. Just as he was about to bite me an enormous lion with a massive mane weighting at least four-hundred pounds, came out and jumped the lion with roars while announcing he is in charge! The larger lion had stopped them from devouring me. He walked over to me and nudged me as I laid on the dirt hill. This large creature seemed to encourage me to get up. Then bowed down in front of me as if he desired me to get on him to ride. The other lions were roaring loud and fiercely there was a message in the roars. I got on the master lion not knowing where he was taking me. I softly said to my Father your praise will continually be in my mouth forever and ever. After about a half-hour ride night was falling and I noticed the camp up ahead and I heard Jessies' voice on a speaker talking to a group of people. He was pretending to cry saying a lion jumped out and grabbed my wife, she is gone my wife is gone.

The closer we got someone spotted us and shouted "look"! Some people ran some stood in shock and could not run due to fear.

Jessie and Art stood in great disbelief and fear, the two guides were next to them.

The main lion stopped then roared and the other lions attacked Jessie, Art, and the two guides. They were killed and drugged to the outside of the camp.

I turned and looked at the main lion and he turned and walked away.

I am convinced beyond a reasonable doubt the words said to me "I am with you always".

Oh, by the way, my name is Victorious!

Rewind

Jessie complained to Art, that he hated being broke. Since his rehab, he could not find work that would pay him what he needed to get the things he deserved and wanted. Jessie was mad his car was sold to pay bills while he was in rehab and he hated his wife for it.

Art asked Jessie how do you think I have all this? Mansion, cars, clothes, fabulous trips, limousines at my discretion?

How Jessie ask? I put a million-dollar insurance policy on my wife's. They are younger than me and no health problems. Using different insurance companies each time and taking them on safaris, no one in the USA is going to question a lion, tiger, or leopard. I pay the tour guides to help and be a witness. Ok Art, Jessie says hook me up.

Art said to Jessie to get the policy and I will make all the plans just get her to go on safari.

Kaylee is next said Art to Jessie. I'll make her stay behind next year is her time. I am thinking of Botswana. Art lights a cigar and laughs.

unapologetically